# Sunny or Cloudy?

Story by Kris Bonnell

Pictures by Alice Bonnell

"Today is going to be sunny,"
said the little frog.

"No," said the big frog.
"Today is going to be cloudy."

"Today is not going
to be cloudy,"
said the little frog.
"Today is going to be sunny."

"Oh, no it is not,"
said the big frog.

"Oh, yes it is,"
said the little frog.

"Oh, no it is not,"
said the big frog.

"Today is not going
to be cloudy,"
said the little frog.

"Today is not going
to be sunny,"
said the big frog.

"Today is going to be rainy,"
they said.